Nature's Fury

DROUGHTS

John Hamilton

Published by ABDO Publishing Company, 4940 Viking Drive, Suite 622, Edina, Minnesota 55435.

Copyright ©2006 by Abdo Consulting Group, Inc. International copyrights reserved in all countries. No part of this book may be reproduced in any form without written permission from the publisher. ABDO & Daughters™ is a trademark and logo of ABDO Publishing Company.

Printed in the United States.

Editor: Paul Joseph

Graphic Design: John Hamilton

Cover Design: Neil Klinepier

Cover Photo: Corbis

Interior Photos and Illustrations:

Corbis, p. 1, 3, 4, 5, 6-7, 8, 9, 12, 13, 15, 16, 18, 19, 20, 21, 22-23, 25, 26, 27, 29

John Hamilton, p. 24

NASA, p. 17 (top & bottom)

National Weather Service, p. 10

Federal Interagency Stream Restoration Working Group, p. 11

Library of Congress Cataloging-in-Publication Data

Hamilton, John, 1959–
     Droughts / John Hamilton.
         p. cm. — (Nature's fury)
     Includes index.
     ISBN 1-59679-329-5
     1. Droughts—Juvenile literature. I. Title.

     QC929.25.H36 2005
     363.34'929—dc22

                                                                2005048083

CONTENTS

In 2002, a drought killed thousands of kangaroos in Australia's Sturt National Park.

SLOW-MOTION DISASTER

WATER—IT'S AS PRECIOUS AS GOLD WHEN A DROUGHT STRIKES.
Sometimes we barely notice when a drought begins, when the water starts drying up.
But with time, the signs become unmistakable. As an arid, dusty wind blows across
the landscape, you begin to feel your throat drying out. Cracks appear in the ground.
Grass, once green, turns brown and shrivels under the hot sun.

As the drought drags on, things start dying. Crops wither in the fields, livestock perish in dust storms, and famine stalks the land—all for lack of water. It's like watching death in slow motion.

When people think of natural disasters, they most often think of sudden calamities like tornados, earthquakes, or floods. Droughts don't begin or end suddenly. They sometimes last for years. When a tornado strikes, you immediately know it. But it's hard to know exactly when a drought begins.

A group of drought-stricken trees.

Most people would say that a drought is what happens when you don't get any rain. But it's a little more complicated than that. Scientists define a drought as when a region gets less rainfall than expected, over a long period of time. It's a fact that some areas of the world

A farmer sits in his dry field in the northern Indian state of Haryana in 2002. That year the entire country experienced its worst drought in recent memory.

naturally get more rain than others. This is a normal climate condition. But a drought can strike anywhere, from the deserts of Utah to the normally wet forests of Oregon. When any area gets less rain than it normally should, it's called a drought. But a drought in Oregon will likely produce more rain than "normal" conditions in Utah. It all depends on where you live, and how water is normally used.

A drought is a normal part of climate. It is not a random event, and it is not rare. It happens everywhere from time to time. Sometimes it lasts only a week or two, and no lasting damage is done. When a severe drought strikes, it can last for years, or decades. Eventually, the rains return, and the weather gets back to normal. How long a drought persists depends on the region in which it strikes. In the Amazon rainforest, it's considered a drought if it doesn't rain after more than a few days. In arid desert climates, it's normal to go weeks without rain.

Even though it is a slow-motion disaster, droughts can be very costly, both in damage and in lives lost. In the United States, people seldom are killed by droughts, but the amount of

A farmer in India sits in the dried up bottom of a lake after a disastrous drought in 2000.

damage can be staggering. The United States Federal Emergency Management Agency (FEMA) estimates that droughts cost Americans an average of $6-8 billion each year. That makes droughts the most damaging of all natural disasters, even worse than hurricanes or tornadoes. We need water for so many activities, from growing food to producing electricity, from washing our cars and dishes to cooling the machines in our factories—not to mention drinking water to sustain our very lives. When the rains refuse to fall, almost everyone is affected somehow.

Severe droughts are killers. They can cause famine and unbelievable suffering. In the United States, the Great Plains and western states have suffered terrible droughts in the past. The most famous period was the 1930s, when the Great Plains were reduced to a parched "Dust Bowl" that wrecked lives and affected the economy of the entire nation. One of the most notorious droughts in modern history happened in Asia in 1877. As many as 40 million people perished in China and India. This monumental disaster led scientists to find the answers to why droughts occur, and how we can better prepare for them.

Did years of severe drought cause the Maya civilization to collapse?

Severe, persistent droughts can even destroy entire cultures. Some archaeologists believe that the great Maya civilization of ancient Mesoamerica collapsed because of a long, crushing drought. Archaeologist Richardson Gill says in his book, *The Great Maya Droughts,* that a 200-year dry period killed millions of Mayans between 800 and 1000 A.D. Gill says that the Maya people's famine and thirst caused their entire civilization to shrink and then finally collapse. It is a mystery why the Maya people could not adjust to their changing climate. Other scientists say additional forces, such as volcanic eruptions and internal political strife, probably combined with the unrelenting drought to bring an end to the Mayans.

A farmer from Bismarck, North Dakota, watches dry soil from a drought-scorched field blow away from his hands.

WHAT CAUSES DROUGHTS?

THE HYDROLOGIC CYCLE IS A PATTERN OF HOW WATER FLOWS on the earth. It's a circular pattern where water travels from oceans to the atmosphere, and then back to the earth. Once on the earth, it goes into the ground, or flows down rivers until it eventually meets the ocean, where the cycle begins all over again.

Water exists in three physical forms: solid ice, liquid water, and gaseous water vapor. When water evaporates, it turns into water vapor. Warm air near the ground rises, carrying the water vapor into the atmosphere. When the vapor hits cold layers of air, it condenses and falls back to the ground as either snow, hail, sleet, or rain.

Masses of air move around the globe in big pockets called high- or low-pressure systems. In a high-pressure weather system, warm air doesn't rise. Since the air isn't rising, it can't take water vapor to the colder levels of the atmosphere. This keeps water vapor from condensing into rain.

High-pressure systems also push clouds and air currents away from an area. If the weather outside is sunny with no clouds, it is probably because of a high-pressure weather

A weather map showing high- and low-pressure systems.

DOMAINE AND WEATHER
PRESSURE AND WEATHER
ISSUED 1603Z SUN JUN 26 2005
VALID: 0000Z MON JUN 27 2005
FORECASTER: BELL

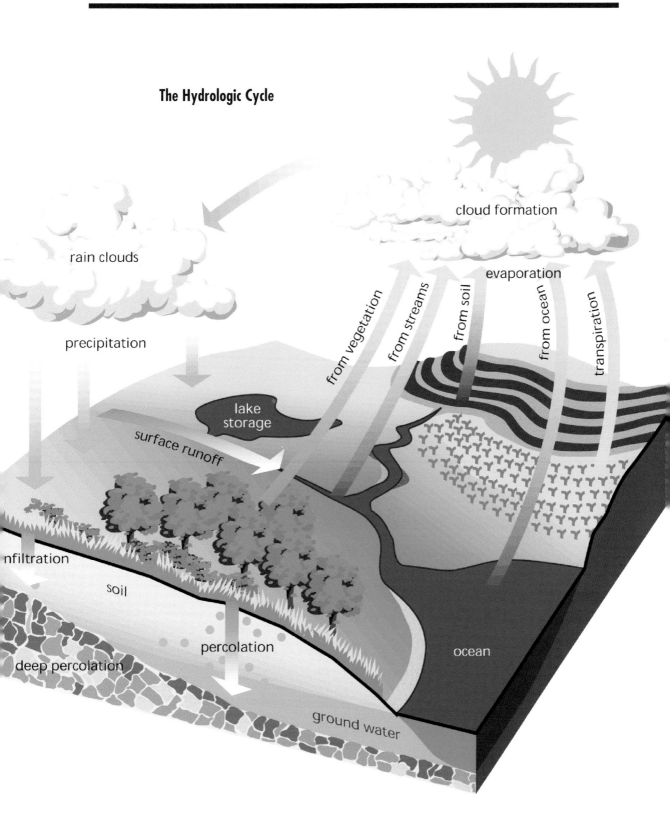

The Hydrologic Cycle

cloud formation

rain clouds

evaporation

precipitation

from vegetation

from streams

from soil

from ocean

transpiration

lake storage

surface runoff

infiltration

soil

percolation

deep percolation

ocean

ground water

This photo, taken from the space shuttle, shows clouds in the jet stream moving over the Red Sea.

system. When a low-pressure system arrives, it brings with it clouds and stormy weather.

Every place in the world has high- and low-pressure weather systems, one after the other. They move around the earth, pushed by big rivers of air in the upper atmosphere called jet streams. Jet streams are very wide, and move up to 335 miles per hour (539 km/hr). They normally have predictable pathways depending on the season. Jet streams sometimes change their normal paths, which can trap high or low-pressure systems over an area, sometimes for days or weeks at a time. When a high-pressure system is stalled over an area, a drought is the usual result.

A drought also happens when normal air currents don't blow the way they're supposed to. Moisture that evaporates from the ocean is taken overland by normal wind patterns. For example, much of the moisture that falls on the eastern U.S. comes from moisture-laden wind from the Gulf of Mexico. Other winds blow this same air to the Midwest. The moisture eventually falls to the ground as rain, which makes it possible to grow crops. Sometimes the winds blow in the wrong direction, or the wrong time, or are too weak. Rains then fall in areas that don't need it, and other areas suffer from droughts.

Unusually warm or cold ocean currents can also disrupt weather systems. When water currents in the Pacific Ocean are warmer than usual, it is called El Niño, a Spanish name that means "the child," a reference to Jesus. Vast, warm pools of hotter-than-normal water are the fuel that storms feed on. Every few years, El Niño appears, and the resulting low-pressure systems bring severe weather to North and South America. Sometimes the water currents are colder than normal. In the Pacific Ocean, this is called La Niña, which means "little girl" in Spanish. These conditions bring droughts.

In Asia, the opposite reaction happens. La Niña brings stormy weather. El Niño interrupts the normal monsoon, or rainy, season. In bad years, millions of people suffer through famine and disease from lack of moisture for crops or clean drinking water.

Mountains can also keep rain from falling on some areas. When air bumps up against tall mountain ranges, it rises, cools, and drops its moisture as rain or snow. By the time the air travels across the range, to the leeward side, it is dried out. That is why so many deserts are found on the leeward sides of mountain ranges. This is a normal climate condition, however, and isn't really considered a drought.

A digital image of the globe, showing El Niño as a white band running horizontally across the Pacific Ocean.

DEFINING DROUGHTS

THERE ARE MANY WAYS TO DEFINE DROUGHTS. A *METEOROLOGICAL drought* happens in places when there is a long period of time with less rain or snow than you expect. Meteorologists are people who study weather and climate. They call this condition a "period of below average precipitation." In non-desert temperate climate zones (between the tropics and the polar circles) a drought is usually classified as 15 days in a row with less than 0.01 inches (0.25 mm) of rain.

An *agricultural drought* happens when there isn't enough rainfall to support crops, or grassy range for livestock. This condition can happen even when there's an average amount of precipitation in an area. Sometimes natural soil conditions, or the way agricultural techniques affect the soil, demand more water than an area naturally receives.

Hydrologic drought happens when water reserves in lakes, reservoirs, and underground aquifers drop below an average level. This can happen even when there is no meteorological drought because of increased human use of the water reserves. Rapidly growing cities, especially in desert climates, sometimes experience hydrologic drought.

The important thing to remember about defining droughts is that they are not purely natural events. The impact of droughts has much to do with human expectations. People place demands on their water supply. If it were possible, people would love to have an unlimited amount of water at their disposal. Sometimes we act as if this was the case, but this attitude usually leads to hardship or disaster.

A woman draws water from a well in a dry riverbed in Kenya, Africa.

Several years of drought conditions have resulted in a drop in the water level of Lake Mead, which can be seen here as a white line along the cliffs.

For example, in Las Vegas, Nevada, many homeowners enjoy having a lawn full of green grass. This cannot occur naturally in the desert climate of Las Vegas, so people irrigate with water. Most of the water is drawn from nearby Lake Mead, which was created by damming the Colorado River. As the city grew at a rapid pace toward the end of the 20th century, it seemed as if Lake Mead would provide an endless supply of water. But after years of drought conditions, coupled with a tremendous growth in population, the lake level began dropping at an alarming rate. In a three-year period, from May 2000 to May 2003, the water dropped more than 60 feet (18 m).

In response to the drought, a thirsty Las Vegas was forced to restrict how much water its citizens could use. People were encouraged to get rid of their lush, green-grass lawns. Instead, people are now replacing grass with "natural" landscaping, including rocks and desert plants. Other restrictions have also been

These two satellite images taken from space show a significant lowering of the water level of Lake Mead. Compare the shoreline of the top image, taken in 2000, with the bottom image, which was taken just three years later.

put in place, such as a ban on fountains and limits on water-guzzling car washes and golf courses.

A similar drought hit the area in the early 1960s. It took 10 years for Lake Mead to recover to its normal water levels. The current drought of the early 2000's seems to be much more severe. Some scientists say it may be the worst drought to hit the region in centuries.

The water level of the Colorado River, which feeds into Lake Mead, is at its lowest point in 100 years. Meanwhile, evaporation and human use continues to drain the lake faster than the Colorado River can replenish it. The effects of the drought are felt not only in the Las Vegas area, but downstream as well. Many other southwestern states, plus northern Mexico, depend on the Colorado River as a lifeline for water.

The change in water level in Lake Mead is very dramatic. But as of 2005, nobody is panicking just yet. There is still plenty of water held in the lake, enough to meet the needs of agriculture and most needs of surrounding cities like Las Vegas. Fluctuations in the lake level are normal, and most people expect the waters to eventually rise once again. When exactly that might occur, nobody can say for sure.

One recent rainfall study hints that the current dry spell may actually be a return to a normal climate. Some scientists think that the southern Nevada area was unusually wet during the past several decades. Only now, they say, is it returning to its regular rainfall pattern. If that's true, then is the area actually in a drought? Perhaps what Las Vegas is experiencing now is "normal."

This shows one reason why it is so hard to define a drought. It is a natural phenomenon, but it is also a measure of human expectations, and how well we manage our water resources.

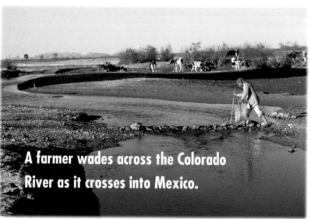

A farmer wades across the Colorado River as it crosses into Mexico.

Rows of houses in a Las Vegas suburb. Years of drought have made it more difficult to maintain non-native, water-dependant lawns.

THE DUST BOWL

IN THE DISASTROUS SUMMER OF 1934, FLORA ROBERTSON WAS A young farmwife scraping a living off the land in Oklahoma. Her family had already suffered through floods, followed by clouds of locusts. Then the rains stopped coming. For several years the drought-stricken land, already overused by wheat farmers using poor conservation techniques, went dry. By 1934, extreme drought affected about 65 percent of the country. The Great Plains turned into a virtual desert. People called it the Dust Bowl.

The worst places hit by the drought included parts of Colorado, New Mexico, Texas, Kansas, and the Oklahoma Panhandle. These areas were originally covered with prairie grasses, which held the soil in place. But new settlers tore up the land, using age-old farming techniques and plowing deep into the ground. Overgrazing by cattle and sheep also harmed the topsoil. When the rains stopped coming, the stage was set for disaster.

An Oklahoma dust storm in 1937.

One windy day in 1934, Flora Robertson looked to the horizon and saw a black cloud coming her way. At first she thought it was the smoke from a train smokestack. Then she realized it was something

A young farm boy covers his nose and mouth against brown sand in the Dust Bowl.

much worse. Like a black, boiling wall hundreds of feet high, the cloud blotted out the sun as it descended on the farm.

"We ran into the storm cellar," she said, "because we thought it was a storm. We lit a lamp, and it was just so dark in there we couldn't see one another… and we just choked and smothered." The cloud was a dust storm, a lung-choking "black blizzard" that raced across the plains, literally blowing away the land.

"My husband was out, after the cows," said Flora, "and he stumbled up against the barbed wire fence, and he followed the fence until he came to the house.… We had to tie wet rags over our mouth just to keep from smothering. We'd get cloths and buckets of water and tie them over our mouths down in the cellar."

Several terrifying hours later, the dust storm blew past. When Flora and her family emerged from the cellar and went into their house, dust and dirt covered all of their belongings. They were forced to use wet mops to swab every square inch of their house. But even more devastating for Flora and other farmers in the area, the crops in their fields were severely damaged. Some fields were completely blown away,

A farm is about to be engulfed by a dust storm during the Dust Bowl of the 1930s.

leaving nothing but raw, seedless dirt behind.

As the drought continued, year after year, dozens of dust storms plagued the people of the Dust Bowl. A bad storm, said Flora, might last half a day. "Sometimes it would be a week before we would see the sun, it was just so darkened." Farm fields from all over the regions were being picked up by the wind and scattered over the countryside. "Sometimes the cloud would look black," said Flora. "Sometimes it would be red. It was according to which way the dirt came, whether it was the red dirt that was blowing over, or the black dirt, according to which way the storm was coming."

No matter how tight they sealed up their homes, the dust storm always left behind coatings of dirt. For livestock caught out in the fields, the storms were deadly. "We had cows," said Flora, "and the storm killed them when they were out in it. (Afterwards) we would cut

their lungs open and it looked just like a mud pack in there."

Flora and her family kept coming back to their farm, trying to rebuild and replant, but after five long years of relentless dust storms, they finally gave up. Like many people in the area, they packed their belongings and moved west in search of work. Many finally settled in California.

By 1935, the situation was so serious that the U.S. government had to find solutions. Dust storms were blowing across the country, sometimes even darkening the skies as far away as Washington, D.C. New farming and conservation methods were developed that helped hold down topsoil in the Dust Bowl region. But even with these steps, the drought persisted, and the disaster continued. The drought lasted about 10 years and brought untold misery. Some experts say it even increased the length of the Great Depression of the 1930s.

DUST STORM DAMAGE, 1930-1940

Montana
North Dakota
South Dakota
Wyoming
Nebraska
Colorado
Kansas
Oklahoma
New Mexico
Texas

Dust Bowl States
Area with most severe dust storm damage
Other areas damaged by dust storms

Photographer Dorothea Lange found this family of Oklahoma drought refugees camping by the roadside near Blythe, California.

PLANNING FOR DROUGHTS

TRYING TO PREDICT WHEN A DROUGHT WILL HAPPEN CAN BE very difficult. Droughts begin and end slowly, unlike other extreme weather events such as tornadoes or hurricanes. To understand when droughts occur, scientists study weather and climate conditions around the world. They try to find connections and patterns in order to predict when the next drought might strike.

Using computer models and historic weather records, some climate researchers now say that large El Niño events can be predicted up to two years ahead of time. If the scientists' research is correct, it could greatly help governments, farmers, and city engineers to plan for droughts or heavy rainfalls. For example, if farmers know a drought is likely in the coming year, they might decide to plant crops that don't need as much water. City planners might decide to store additional water supplies, or conserve water in advance by restricting water use by citizens.

Soil bakes under a hot sun during a drought.

Some scientists say there is a connection between drought cycles and sunspots, which are cooler areas that appear as black spots on the surface of the sun. Sunspots and the drought cycles of many regions

A farmer holds a handful of dried soil. Some crops grow better in dry conditions. If future drought forecasts become more accurate, farmers will be able to better plan which crops to plant.

each seem to occur every 22 years. No direct proof has been found, but some scientists believe that increased solar activity somehow causes slight changes to our atmosphere, altering it just enough to cause an increased chance of droughts.

It's often hard to tell when you're in a drought, especially when it's just beginning. Scientists try to accurately track droughts by watching certain clues. These measurements include water levels in rivers and streams, the amount of soil moisture, and the amount of rainfall or snow that an area has recently had.

The North American Drought Monitor is a map showing weekly drought conditions in the United States, Canada, and Mexico. It is produced by scientists from several government agencies, including the National Drought Mitigation Center, the U.S. Department of Agriculture, and the National Oceanic and Atmospheric Administration. The maps use data from satellites, news accounts, ground measurements, and eyewitness accounts to show where a drought is happening, and how severe it is.

There are steps people can take to prepare for droughts, or to reduce their impact. These actions are called *drought mitigation*. Mitigation mainly involves finding more water supplies, and conserving the water we already have.

One way of creating better supplies of water is to build dams. These big reservoirs of water can be tapped even in times of drought, or used to store excess water when the weather is unusually rainy. This spreads out the impact of rain/drought cycles. There are about 75,000 large dams in the United States.

Aquifers are large underground lakes that hold a lot of water. Some aquifers are gigantic. The Ogallala Aquifer lies under the states of South Dakota, Nebraska, Oklahoma, Texas, and Kansas. Aquifers can be reached by drilling. Water piped up from an aquifer can be used to irrigate crops, or for drinking water for cities.

There is always a danger of too much human activity threatening an aquifer. Sometimes so much is pumped out that its level drops, threatening an entire region's water supply. Also, there is a risk of contaminants, such as pesticides or toxic chemicals, reaching an aquifer, making the water unsafe for drinking.

Other ways of finding additional water supplies in time of drought included the construction of canals and pipelines, and desalination plants, which take the salt out of seawater and make it useable for human needs.

Water conservation is an important way of making scarce water supplies last longer during times of drought. New showers, toilets, and washing machines use much less water today, sometimes cutting usage in half. Farmers use special sprinkler or drip irrigation systems to save huge amounts of water. Water recycling programs conserve by reusing water. For example, some cities treat their wastewater, which is then reused on golf courses or city parks.

People are constantly finding new ways to conserve. Some methods are very simple, but save a surprisingly large amount of water. For example, a water park in Denver called Water World decided to stop putting ice cubes in drinks it sold at concession stands. This simple step saved about 30,000 gallons of water each year.

By conserving water and finding more efficient ways of using this precious resource, most areas can survive the onslaught of a severe drought. But if water is wasted, or the land used in inappropriate ways, a sun-baked drought will likely lead to disaster.

At long last, a rain shower breaks a drought, sending much-needed water to this farm.

GLOSSARY

Agricultural Drought

When there isn't enough rainfall to support crops, or grassy range for livestock.

Climate

The average weather conditions of a place. Climate is determined by adding up temperature and other weather events, such as rain, over a period of years. A dry period of a few weeks doesn't necessarily mean an area has a dry climate. A weather condition has to persist for years before it is considered part of an area's climate. One of the difficulties in identifying global warming is deciding if increased temperatures are merely isolated weather events, or part of a larger climate-changing event.

Drought Mitigation

Steps that people can take to prepare for droughts, or reduce their impact. Mitigation involves finding more water supplies, such as building reservoirs or tapping aquifers, or by conserving water.

El Niño

A weather pattern that is created when water currents in the Pacific Ocean are warmer than usual. In North and South America, this usually brings severe weather. In Asia, El Niño often results in droughts.

Hydrologic Cycle

The pattern of how water flows and recycles on the earth. Liquid water from oceans and lakes evaporates, forming clouds. When rain falls to the ground, it travels down rivers and streams until it eventually meets the ocean, where the cycle begins again.

Hydrologic Drought

When water reserves in lakes, reservoirs, and underground aquifers drop below an average level.

Jet Stream

A large stream of air in the upper atmosphere. Jet streams have a predictable pathway, depending on the season. If a jet stream changes its normal path, it can trap high- or low-pressure weather systems over a region. If a high-pressure system is stalled over an area, droughts are usually the result.

La Niña

A weather pattern that is created when water currents in the Pacific Ocean are colder than usual. In North and South America, this usually results in droughts. In Asia, La Niña often results in more severe weather than usual.

Meteorological Drought

When there is a long period of time with less rain or snow than is expected.

Meteorologist

Someone who studies the weather and climate patterns.

WEB SITES

WWW.ABDOPUB.COM

Would you like to learn more about droughts? Please visit www.abdopub.com to find up-to-date Web site links about droughts and other natural disasters. These links are routinely monitored and updated to provide the most current information available.

INDEX